Dedication

Mommy, you mean the world to me your strength is courageous. Keep smiling!

In memory of my Daddy (Westside Barber), thank you for waiting to say our goodbyes. You will always be my rock.

Calvin, I could not do this without your love and continued support. It may not always be said, but it's never forgotten.

Tyra, my sunshine, your hard work and diligence encourages me to be a better me.

Aaron, if it wasn't for your creativeness and intelligence, I wouldn't have a story to write.

Val, ALWAYS making me laugh until I cry.

Tanya, inspiring me to dream.

Melissa, my confidant, my shoulder, my bestie.

Armani, those wet kisses and utter excitement when I come in the door even if I'm only gone five minutes is the best.

Copyright © 2015

Written by Tracey Strong

Illustrated by Dodot Asmoro

Visit my website at www.alienimagination.co and www.alienimagination.org
First Printed September 2015

ISBN 978-1-68222-037-5

BOOOMM!

1

"What was that?" Jenny asked.

"Look up there," I said.

"Could it really be Sophie?" Jenny asked.

"I don't know. Let's go and find out!" I yelled.

"Sophie, you know we can't leave this area. If Principal Lesowitz finds out, we could get in big trouble."

We'll be back before anyone notices. I promise," I said.

I pleaded with Jenny and then reminded her of the time when she threw a snowball at Timothy Greinberger and I took the blame for it. I missed two recesses, and I had to have a note signed by my parents telling them what I had done.

"Okay Sophie," Jenny said.

We ran as fast as we could while
hiding along bushes to make sure no one saw us.
And as we got closer towards the trees that
stood high above the playground
area, our eyes were blinded by those bright colorful lights. What
happened next made both our mouths drop and our legs tremble
as we looked on in amazement.

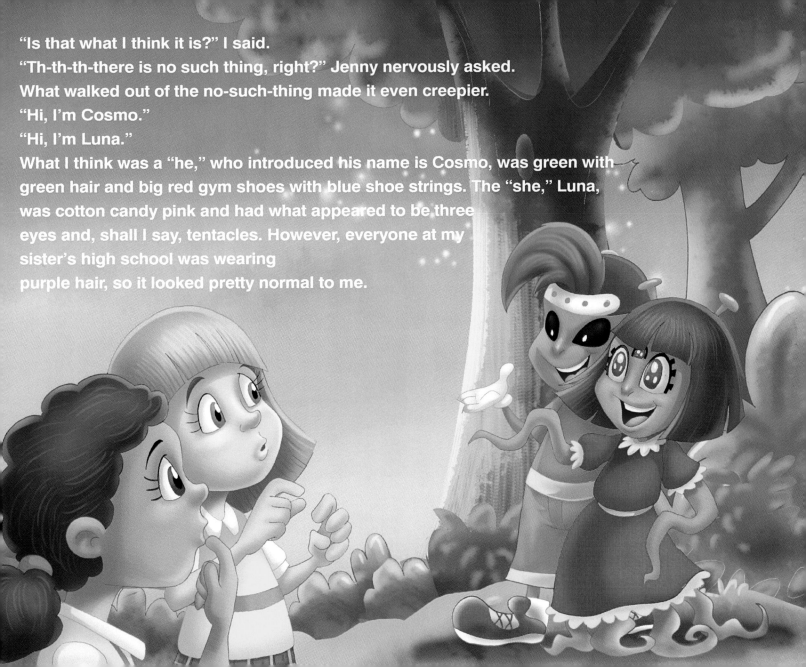

"Is that what I think it is?" I said.

"Th-th-th-there is no such thing, right?" Jenny nervously asked.

What walked out of the no-such-thing made it even creepier.

"Hi, I'm Cosmo."

"Hi, I'm Luna."

What I think was a "he," who introduced his name is Cosmo, was green with green hair and big red gym shoes with blue shoe strings. The "she," Luna, was cotton candy pink and had what appeared to be three eyes and, shall I say, tentacles. However, everyone at my sister's high school was wearing purple hair, so it looked pretty normal to me.

"I-I-I'm Jenny, and this is my friend, umh uhm uhm" she said.

"Sorry for my friend, but I'm Sophie, and are you like, really like, aliens?

"Be quiet," Jenny said softly.

"It's okay. We really are aliens," Luna said as she used
her tentacles to smooth her hair.

So cool, I was thinking to myself.

"What brings you here?" I said.

"We are from the planet Gitar," Cosmo stated.

"Guitar?" I asked.

"No, Gitar. We have been learning about the planet Earth in our school for many years, and we just needed to see it for ourselves," Luna said with a bright smile.

Cosmo loved science and read everything from Alien Report and Science News to Sports Illustrated. He was most fascinated to learn about the people on Earth. He created an electronic device he called IWARE, made out of small pieces of Meteorites that had fallen onto their planet, which allowed him to hear and see us millions of miles away. This is how they were able to emulate us so well.

"Wow!" My mom wouldn't even let me go to the bus stop by myself," said Jenny. And she was serious. Her mom still walked her to the bus stop, which was only half of a block from her house, and held her hand every morning, and we were going into the 3rd grade next school year.

We all burst into laughter, which made everyone feel a little more at ease.

15

"Oh no, Sophie! We need to get back immediately. We only have three minutes left until our recess is over," Jenny exclaimed.

"Our next recess is at 12:30. Can you meet us at the playground area that is right behind our school?" I asked.

"We would love to!" said Luna.

"Great, see you soon," I said.

"One minute left Sophie!" Jenny yelled.

"I don't think we are going to make it in time!" I screamed.

17

"Whew, that was close," Jenny said.

18

Luna was so excited to visit earth because back home Luna wasn't an avid reader like her friend Cosmo, but she loved to watch all the latest fashions that all the girls wore on his IWARE. One day she created her own skinny jeans for her and her best friend, Gala. They thought they looked stunning.

The following day when Cosmo and Luna entered the playground, all the kids looked directly at them and stared; luckily, they had gotten pretty used to "the stare." However, they still weren't quite sure what to do about it. The news had already spread throughout school about our new friends, and to be honest, not too many people believed it.

But there was only one student who seemed upset by it, and that was Jerimiah Flanagan. He had won the spelling bee, math counts and had taken 1st place every year in the science fair. He was the smartest kid in our school and he knew it. Jerimiah wanted to make sure everyone in school knew it, too. But because he had read in Readers Digest that aliens have a high IQ, he thought if aliens were allowed to enroll, that he would no longer be known as the smartest kid in our school.

Everyone gathered around to play jump rope. First up was Jasmine, a 2nd grader, who loved to wear her hair in a ponytail and flowery socks every day. While Jasmine was jumping, Jenny and Sophie on each end were twirling the rope and everyone was singing in chorus: "Icecream soda pop cherry on top, who is your best friend let's find out: Go A, B, C, D, E, F." Jasmine finally missed, so next it was Cosmo's turn.

"Icecream soda pop cherry on top, who is your best friend let's find out: Go A, B, C, D, E, F, G, H, J, K, L, M, N, O, P, Q, R, S, T, U, V, W, X, Y, Z." Cosmo not only could jump high, he could do turns and then while the rope was twirling he did a head spin on the floor as if he was break dancing. It was the coolest move ever! Everyone cheered for Cosmo.

However, it wasn't surprising because back home Cosmo was a great athlete and loved to show off all his spinning moves on the basketball court when they would have play time.

Next it was Luna's turn:

"Icecream so-"

"Oh-oh, try again, Luna," said Sophie.

"Icecream."

Luna's tentacles were moving all over the place, and she kept missing as she attempted to jump. Then all of a sudden, she landed splat on the concrete with her tentacles intertwined in the ropes. Luna was okay, but she was really embarrassed as Cosmo immediately came to her rescue. Everyone burst into uncontrollable laughter as we watched Luna get her balance.

"You looked so funny trying to jump," cried Zachary.
"How could you be so mean," I shouted. And without saying good bye,
Luna and Cosmo started walking towards their spacecraft. When the other kids
and I realized what had happened, we immediately went to follow them.
"Luna, I am very sorry." Zachary apologized.
Everyone apologized almost in chorus. "That's okay. I just really
wanted to be like everyone else." Luna said sadly.

"We all think your tentacles are awesome," Jenny said.

"Really?" Luna said with excitement.

"Yep, we sure do," everyone exclaimed.

"Would you like to turn Luna?" said Jenny.

"Yes," Luna said happily.

Everyone was so amazed because not only was Luna able to turn, she was turning her tentacles all at once, and everyone got a chance to jump over them at the same time.

Everybody started chanting, "Luna! Luna! Luna! Luna!"
"We had so much fun today; however, it's time for us to go back
home so we can share with our friends our time here on Earth,"
Cosmo said as everyone was waving good- bye. Those bright
lights that bothered our eyes before were blinding our eyes
once again, but it was mega cool to watch.

As we returned back to school, we hadn't realized that the bell had already rung. We quickly headed towards our classroom and took to our seats. Ms. Brown was busy writing our math problem for the day at the board and didn't notice that we had come in.

Knock, knock, knock. The door opened and a short, balding man with horn-rim glasses and a black suit walked in our direction. "Excuse me Ms. Morgain for interrupting your class, but I need to have Sophie and Jenny to please come down to my office immediately," said Principal Lesowitz.

We are doomed, I thought to myself. I could see out the corner of my eyes that Jenny was giving me her look of evil, but I pretended that I wasn't looking her way. I already knew this was all my fault, and I started to feel really bad inside. As we entered Principal Lesowitz's office, we prepared for the worst.

"Girls, I just wanted to remind you that you are signed up for patrol monitoring at 8:15 tomorrow morning. Here are your badges, and please make sure you come to the main office to sign in. Thank you for volunteering girls."

"Is that it, Mr. Lesowitz?" I said with doubt.

"Yes, unless you have any other questions or concerns." Jenny didn't say a word, and she looked pretty relieved by what just happened. Finally, I was able to take a breath and thank my lucky stars that we weren't in any trouble after all.

PRINCIPAL LESOWITZ

As I glanced out of Principal Lesowitz's office window, I could still see their spaceship high above the trees, slowly dissipating into the sky. I looked forward to one day seeing our new friends, Cosmo and Luna, again and wondered how we would spend our time together.